P9-CBE-299

The Mystery at

Big Ben

by Carole Marsh

CHICAGO HEIGHTS PUBLIC LIBRARY

Copyright ©2006 Carole Marsh/ Gallopade International
All rights reserved.
First Edition

3-5
a/

Carole Marsh Mysteries™ and its skull colophon are the
property of Carole Marsh and Gallopade International.

Published by Gallopade International/Carole Marsh Books.
Printed in the United States of America.

Managing Editor: Sherry Moss
Cover Design: Michele Winkelman

Picture Credits:

The publisher would like to thank the following for their kind permission to
reproduce the cover photographs.

Kevin Connors, Clifton, New Jersey *London Guard;*
© Simon Gurney | Agency: Dreamstime.com *London Eye;*
© 2005 JupiterImages Corporation *Big Ben; Suit of Armor*

Gallopade is proud to be a member and supporter of these
educational organizations and associations:
International Reading Association
National Association for Gifted Children
The National School Supply and Equipment Association
The National Council for the Social Studies
Museum Store Association
Association of Partners for Public Lands

Without limiting the rights under copyright reserved above, no part of this
publication may be reproduced, stored in or introduced into a retrieval system, or
transmitted, in any form or by any means (electronic, mechanical, photocopying,
recording or otherwise), without the prior written permission of both the copyright
owner and the above publisher of this book.

The scanning, uploading, and distribution of this book via the Internet or via any
other means without the permission of the publisher is illegal and punishable by
law. Please purchase only authorized electronic editions and do not participate in or
encourage electronic piracy of copyrightable materials. Your support of the author's
rights is appreciated.

20 Years Ago . . .

As a mother and an author, one of the fondest periods of my life was when I decided to write mystery books for children. At this time (1979) kids were pretty much glued to the TV, something parents and teachers complained about the way they do about web surfing and blogging today.

I decided to set each mystery in a real place—a place kids could go and visit for themselves after reading the book. And I also used real children as characters. Usually a couple of my own children served as characters, and I had no trouble recruiting kids from the book's location to also be characters.

Also, I wanted all the kids—boys and girls of all ages—to participate in solving the mystery. And, I wanted kids to learn something as they read. Something about the history of the location. And I wanted the stories to be funny. That formula of real+scary+smart+fun served me well.

I love getting letters from teachers and parents who say they read the book with their class or child, then visited the historic site and saw all the places in the mystery for themselves. What's so great about that? What's great is that you and your children have an experience that bonds you together forever. Something you shared. Something you both cared about at the time. Something that crossed all age levels—a good story, a good scare, a good laugh!

20 years later,

Carole Marsh

2-5-07 Daisy 14.99

Christina
"Mystery Girl"
Mimi Papa
Grant

About the Characters

 **Christina**, age 10: Mysterious things really do happen to her! Hobbies: soccer, Girl Scouts, anything crafty, hanging out with Mimi, and going on new adventures.

 **Grant**, age 7: Always manages to fall off boats, back into cactuses, and find strange clues—even in real life! Hobbies: camping, baseball, computer games, math, and hanging out with Papa.

 **Mimi** is Carole Marsh, children's book author and creator of Carole Marsh Mysteries, Around the World in 80 Mysteries, Three Amigos Mysteries, Baby's First Mysteries, and many others.

 **Papa** is Bob Longmeyer, the author's real-life husband, who really does wear a tuxedo, cowboy boots and hat, fly an airplane, captain a boat, speak in a booming voice, and laugh a lot!

Travel around the world with Christina and Grant as they visit famous places in 80 countries, and experience the mysterious happenings that always seem to follow them!

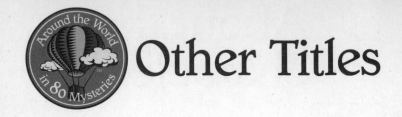

Other Titles

#1   The Mystery at Big Ben

#2   The Mystery at the Eiffel Tower

#3   The Mystery at the Roman Colosseum

#4   The Mystery of the Golden Pyramid

Table of Contents

1 Getting There is Half the Fun. 1

2 Puttin' on the Ritz. 7

3 Big Red Bus. 15

4 Big Ben 21

5 The Eye in the Sky 25

6 Jet Lag 31

7 Warned! 39

8 Teddy Bears and Tooth Brushes. 45

9 Scotland Yard. 47

10 The Infamous Tower of London 53

11 Skip to M'loo, My Darlin' 59

12 Showing Your Hand. 63

13 Piccadilly Circus 67

14 Cleopatra's Needle 75

15 To Be or Not to Be 83

16 221b Baker Street. 89

17 Run!. 93

18 Her Majesty, the Queen! 101

19 Last Warning!. 109

20 Trick...or Treat?. 115

21 Saved by the Bell! 121

22 Elementary, My Dear Watson! 125

About the Series Creator 131

Write Your Own Mystery. 132

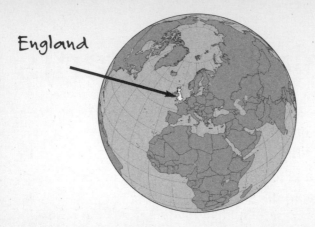

England

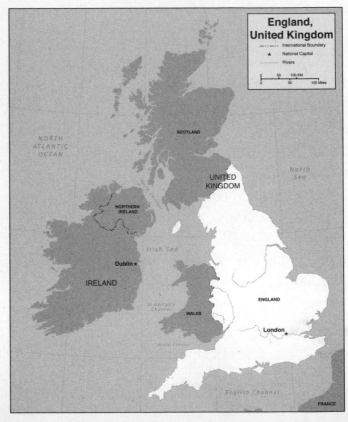

Getting There is Half the Fun

"*BONG! BONG!*" cried Grant. "*BONG...BONG...BONG...BONG!*"

"Grant, if you *bong* one more time, I'm going to *bong* you on the head," his grandmother Mimi said.

They were standing in the middle of busy Heathrow Airport watching for Papa and Grant's sister Christina to appear with the luggage. They had just flown in from Paris aboard Papa's little red and white airplane, *The Mystery Girl*.

Suddenly, an overflowing luggage cart appeared. It staggered left and right toward them as if propelled by a seasick ghost.

Grant jumped just before the cart ran over his

foot. "Hey, careful there!" he screeched.

A head thrust out from each side of the cart. "I can't believe we have so much luggage," Papa said. He looked handsome in the cowboy hat and boots and leather vest he always wore, but he was panting like a dog.

Christina plopped down on the floor. "This luggage cart is crazy. I thought we'd never get this stuff pushed all the way over here. I'm exhausted!"

"BONG! BONG! BONG!" cried Grant yet again.

Christina and Papa stared at him like he was crazy. "And just what is that all about?" Papa asked, holding his head with both hands.

Mimi sighed. "Grant thinks he will just die if we don't go see Big Ben right away," she explained. "I do not know why he is so excited about a clock."

Grant thrust his hands on his hips in his don't-make-fun-of-me-just-cause-I'm-only-seven pose. "It isn't just any old clock," he said. "Big Ben is the most famous clock in the world. It's tall and it's loud and I want to see it."

"I doubt that it's as loud as you," Christina teased her brother. She brushed her bangs away from her forehead.

"I doubt anything's as loud as Grant," Papa agreed.

"He's loud, but he's cute and sweet," Mimi said, tousling Grant's blond crewcut, "but I'm still going to *bong* him on the head if he imitates Big Ben anymore till we go and see it for ourselves."

"*Bong...bong...*" whispered Grant.

"What's that?" Christina asked.

"LITTLE BEN!" Grant cried and laughed.

Papa ended the discussion by saying, "Here, pard'ner!" and dumping a large duffle bag into Grant's arms.

"*Ufgh!*" said Grant, swaying under the weight. He wandered left and right. All you could see was the bag and his little arms holding on for dear life and his legs quivering beneath him.

Christina laughed until Papa said, "You, too, Missy!" and tossed her a suitcase that seemed to weigh a ton.

"These are too heavy!" Christina complained.

"Then next time don't pack so much," said Papa. "Those are *your* bags, you know." Papa threw a hanging bag over his shoulder and picked up a small case. "And these are mine," he said with a smile.

Grant had dropped his duffle to the floor. Christina did the same. "Then whose are all those?!" they asked, pointing to a large mound of bright red suitcases of all sizes.

Papa looked at Mimi. Christina looked at Mimi. Grant looked at Mimi. Mimi looked at the ceiling ignoring them all.

"Mimi!" Christina squealed. "What is all that stuff?"

Mimi looked at them and smiled secretively. "Oh, you know. This and that. I do have to meet the Queen, you know. And I have to write a mystery, you know. So, you know, I need a lot of stuff."

Papa just shook his head tiredly. Christina and Grant laughed. Mimi wrote mystery books for kids and set them in real locations, like the one she would be working on here in London, England. Papa was "travel agent" and "trail boss." And when Christina and Grant were out of school, they got to tag along, and were supposed to stay out of the way...but they never did! Why? Because they felt it was their official job to help Mimi discover mysterious facts and places and people to put in her books.

But sometimes, things backfired. Like now? For suddenly, there was a loud BOOM which echoed throughout the busy terminal.

"What was that?" said Mimi.

"Was it a bomb?" Christina asked. She knew there had been some terrorist bombs in London in the past.

"No!" said Grant. "It's that!"

They all turned around and stared at the overloaded luggage cart which had tipped and fallen over, tossing all of Mimi's red luggage to the floor.

"Ufgh!" said Papa with a sigh and began to hoist all the suitcases back into place.

Puttin' on the Ritz

Soon, Mimi, Papa, Grant, and Christina...and all that luggage...were speeding from the airport into downtown London in a shiny, black taxicab.

"Excuse me," said Grant, as soon as they got underway. "EXCUSE ME!" he repeated more urgently.

Finally, the taxi driver realized that Grant was talking to him.

"Yes, son?" he said in an English accent that Christina just loved.

Grant looked very nervous. "In case you didn't notice, I think you're driving on the wrong side of the road!"

The driver just laughed. "Not at all," he

promised. "We drive on the left side of the road in England," he explained. "The left side is the right side to us."

Grant frowned. "The left side is the right side? I think the left side is the wrong side!"

Papa put his arm around his grandson's shoulder. "It's ok, Grant. They really do drive on this side of the road here. You knew that, didn't you, Christina?"

Christina let out a big sigh of relief. "Uh, s-s-sure," she answered. She was three years older than her brother and liked to think that she knew three years' more worth of stuff than he did. But this was a new one. Oh, well, she guessed she'd get used to driving on the wrong side of the road. She wondered why Mimi—who was a scaredy-cat driver and rider—was not saying anything. But when she looked at her grandmother, she understood. Mimi had her eyes closed!

"Where are we headed, sir?" the driver asked Papa.

Papa beamed. He loved to surprise Mimi. "Why to the Ritz, of course!"

Mimi's eyes flew open and she gave Papa a big kiss. "Oh, what fun!" she said. "If we can't stay at Buckingham Palace with the Queen, we might as well stay at the Ritz, right?"

Grant and Christina clung tightly to their jumpseats as the taxi rattled down the busy roads.

"Right!" said Christina.

"Left?" said Grant. "We're here," said Papa and the taxicab swerved neatly into a place in front of a large, magnificent hotel. "THE RITZ!"

* * *

A man in a swanky uniform with gold braided trim opened the taxi's door, doffed his top hat, and escorted Christina onto a red carpet with a swoop of his other arm. "Welcome to the Ritz, young lady!" he said.

"Thank you!" Christina said with surprise.

Soon, they were all parading into the beautiful old hotel which seemed to be all velvet and gold and palm trees and light.

"Wow, Papa," Christina said. "I think you've outdone yourself this time!"

Papa leaned down and whispered, "Maybe I can keep Mimi out of trouble if she can hole up here and write for awhile." He gave his granddaughter a big wink.

Hmm, Christina thought. And maybe if Mimi is writing and Papa is sitting in some big armchair drinking coffee and reading his newspapers like he always does, she and Grant could get out and explore all by themselves like they loved to do.

Mimi led the way down the red carpet like she was a queen. She loved glamour and parties and ritzy places like the Ritz. Their burden of luggage magically vanished and so they paraded right up some thickly-carpeted steps into the beautiful Palm Court for a traditional English afternoon tea.

"I'm not too crazy about tea, you know?" Grant complained.

"Then how about a milkshake, young man?" a waiter said as he seated Grant in a large, overstuffed armchair.

"How about some of those, too!" said Grant, staring hungrily at a mountain of dainty tea sandwiches and mounds and mounds of cookies and pastries.

"Our wish is your command!" said the waiter smartly, as everyone was seated at the beautifully set table.

"I like this puttin' on the ritz," Grant said and

everyone laughed.

Suddenly, a tall, well-dressed (Mimi would say dapper) man strode directly to their table. Without a word he lifted Mimi's hand and kissed the top of it. "Welcome to London!" he said cheerily.

Mimi blushed and introduced him all around. She told them Mr. Byron was the publisher of her books for all of Great Britain which included England, Ireland, Scotland, and all parts of the British Empire, as he called it.

As the man sat down in one of the empty chairs, Grant asked him. "What language do you speak?"

The man laughed. "Why, English, of course!"

"It sounds very different," said Christina.

"They probably speak left English and we speak right English?" guessed Grant.

"We speak the Queen's English," the man said. "The language of the Bard!"

"The Bard?" repeated Grant, confused.

Christina raised her hand as if she were in school. "Oh, you know, Grant...Shakespeare, the play writer."

Grant was still confused. "Did he write the Harry Potter books?"

Everyone laughed and Grant looked like his feelings were hurt. Mimi, who took kids and reading and writing very seriously, set things straight. "William Shakespeare. He is the greatest playwright of all time. He wrote *Romeo and Juliet*, *Twelfth Night*, *Macbeth*, and many other comedies and tragedies."

Suddenly, Grant's eyes lit up. "Oh, yeah! Bill S. I remember him! We studied him in Montessori." He looked like he felt much better.

What Grant really remembered, Christina knew, was that Mimi had written a kids' book about Shakespeare and read it to Grant when he was little. Grant had a very good memory, especially when it came to numbers, which is why, she figured, he was so interested in Big Ben.

"TO BE...OR NOT TO BE...THAT IS THE QUESTION!" Grant blurted, then added: "To be hungry, or to eat some of this good tea stuff—please!"

Everyone laughed and began to fill their plates when two children suddenly ran into the Palm Court. Mr. Byron stood up to greet them.

"May I introduce my own two grandchildren— Maggie and George!" he said proudly. The boy actually gave a bow and the girl curtsied.

Christina and Grant giggled. "Can you teach me to do that?" Christina asked the red-headed, freckle-cheeked girl who looked just her age.

"Oh, you'll have to learn to curtsy if you're going to visit the Queen!" Maggie said. "I'll be glad to teach you." She plopped down into the chair next to Christina. Christina knew they'd be instant friends.

Grant and George, who were also similar ages, stared at one another suspiciously. "You're not going to teach me to bow, are you?" Grant asked.

George, who had pitch black hair slicked back almost like a little vampire, gave a mischievous grin. "Absolutely not," he said. "I'm going to teach you all about torture, rats, and other good stuff."

Grant grinned right back and the two boys shook hands, not even noticing that they were smushing one of the pastries on Grant's plate. Christina could see that they would be instant best friends, too. And as soon as they had eaten, she was eager to let the mystery adventure begin!

Big Red Bus

It didn't take long for the adventure to begin...nor the mystery! Christina was delighted when Mr. Byron said that he had a nephew who drove one of the famous, big, red, double-decker sightseeing buses. He had arranged an afternoon tour for the kids to ride all around London while Mimi and Papa got settled at the Ritz. Christina knew Mimi was on a tight deadline to finish the first draft of her new manuscript and figured her publisher thought if he could get the kids out of her hair, she could settle down and write.

Papa, who was very protective, was a little skeptical. "Is your nephew responsible? Will he keep a good eye on the kids? They do have a tendency to strike out on their own whenever they get a chance," he admitted, giving Grant and Christina a you'd-better-behave look.

"Oh, yes," said Mr. Byron, "this afternoon run is his last of the day and he can drop them off right back here at the Ritz in an hour or so." Just then, the red bus pulled up out front—it was hard to miss!

"Please, Papa?" Christina begged.

'"PLEASSSSSSSSE!" pleaded Grant.

Mimi and Papa looked at each other and nodded and the four kids took off like a streak out of the Palm Court, back down the red carpet, out the revolving door, and up onto the top level of the bus. Mr. Byron had a few words with his nephew, Gilbert. Gilbert shook his head up and down, the two men shook hands, and Mr. Byron joined Mimi and Papa on the red carpet. The kids waved goodbye as the big red bus rolled away.

* * *

What Mr. Byron could not have known is that his nephew Gilbert was going to get off early to go to a rock concert with his girlfriend, Britta, or at least that's what he said. At the very next stop, a new driver came to replace him. Gilbert hopped off the bus and ripped his cap from his head to reveal a lime green Mohawk haircut. Britta, in a short skirt and even shorter top gave him a big hug. "You guys behave, ok?" Gilbert hollered up to the kids. Christina knew Mimi and Papa would not be happy about this, but she did not know what to do. Besides, the new driver immediately pulled out into the busy traffic and they were off!

Soon, Christina was excited and relaxed. It was a beautiful afternoon! The sky was as blue as could be with green-leafed trees swaying in the breeze and a golden afternoon light keeping them warm in their perch on top of the bus.

As they drove around the city of London, the driver kept up a running commentary about the tourist sites. He called off famous names that Christina had heard about, read about, or studied in school. It made her want to stop and visit each place.

"We can do that," said Maggie when Christina expressed her desire aloud. "This is the kind of bus you can get off of at the stops, then reboard later."

"Yeah," said George. "That's the whole idea."

Christina frowned. "I don't think that was Mimi's and Papa's idea." She felt sure her grandparents thought that they would just ride the route and then return to the hotel.

But all of a sudden, the driver called out "BIG BEN!" and Grant, who had been listening to the discussion, jumped up and bounced down the steps and hopped off the bus onto the sidewalk. There was nothing else for the other kids to do but follow him.

As they stood in front of the tall clock tower, Christina and Grant were surprised to hear Maggie say, "That is not Big Ben."

"Sure it is!" said Grant, his ready-to-pick-a-fight look on his face. "It's tall. It's a clock. It's in London. It's Big Ben."

"No, it isn't," Maggie insisted as the kids all stared up at the four-sided clock tower that rose over the Houses of Parliament. "It's the big bell that chimes that is really 'Big Ben'—this is the clock tower."

"Ohhhhh," said Christina, truly surprised.

"Oh," Grant said, truly disappointed. Then he asked, "But I can still call the whole kit-and-kaboodle Big Ben?"

Maggie and George laughed. "Sure!" they

said. "Everybody does!"

"People love Big Ben," Maggie said. "I guess you could say it is one of our most beloved national treasures. This big, old clock has been keeping time since 1859. They even ring the chimes each day on our BBC radio station."

Suddenly, Christina had the strangest feeling. She couldn't help herself. She thought of the World Trade Towers in New York City. Mimi and Papa had taken her and Grant there to ride the elevators of the tall building and see how beautiful the city of Manhattan was at night from the very top floor. In 2001, when terrorists had flown airplanes into the buildings and caused them to collapse, she just couldn't believe it.

She looked up at Big Ben and could see why Grant was so enthralled. The clock tower was glowing like molten copper in the late afternoon sunlight. She sure hoped nothing ever happened to this special and historic clock.

All of a sudden, all the kids jumped! *BONG! BONG! BONG! BONG! BONG!* The clock chimed five-o'clock and all the kids could do was hold their sides and laugh.

Then Grant stopped laughing. He walked right up to the clock tower and ran his hand over the bricks. He looked and looked.

"What is it, Grant?" Christina asked. He was acting very strange and serious. She could not imagine what the problem was.

Grant did not say anything. He continued to stare at the bricks. The other kids peered over his shoulder. They could see a faint sketch done in pencil over several of the bricks. It just looked like doodling to them, but Grant continued to run his hand over the lines and mutter to himself.

"Grant, for heaven's sake, what is it?" Christina asked again. "You're giving me the creeps."

Grant turned around and looked at the kids. "Someone's going to blow up Big Ben," he said. He pointed at the sketch on the wall. "This proves it."

Big Ben

"Oh, Grant," said Christina. "Don't be so silly!" She thought maybe her thoughts had rubbed off on her brother, but she didn't actually believe that Big Ben was in any trouble.

"You shouldn't say things like that," said Maggie. "The bobbies in London take talk like that very seriously. You could get in trouble."

"The bobbies?" said Grant.

"What you call police," George explained. He was like Grant and watched as much television as he was allowed...and then some.

"But look," said Grant. "It's a sketch of the clock tower. But I don't know what this little square is." He pointed to a tiny square in the center of a larger square.

"That's just a box," said George. "Not a tower."

Grant read off some numbers written faintly around the edges of the box. "That's because the sketch is just of the base of the clock tower. But I still can't figure out what this little box inside is," he said, puzzled.

"Maybe it's the cell?" said George.

"What cell?!" the girls asked at the same time.

"There's a little cell room in the top of the tower," George said.

"No way," said his sister. "If there was, I'd know about it. I'm the history buff, you know."

"But I'm the one who likes cells, and dungeons, and stuff like that," argued George.

Christina could see that big sisters and little brothers were alike in any country. "Look, let's don't argue. Grant, your idea seems pretty preposterous. I think we should just go sightsee like we're supposed to. Mimi is in charge of mysteries, and even she doesn't put bombs and real bad stuff in her books. Someone was just doodling, probably drawing something perfectly innocent while they waited for a bus."

Grant looked at his sister and shrugged his shoulders. He muttered to himself, "The math proves it." Christina did not hear him. But she did hear this: "CAN WE RIDE THAT???!!!"

Grant pointed up into the sky over the Thames River which runs through London. Just coming to light in the early evening sky was the giant Eye in the Sky—an enormous Ferris wheel erected for London's 2000 millennium celebration.

Maggie laughed. "I just happen to have four tickets in my back pocket!" she surprised them by saying. "Dad said you might want to ride it sometime while you were here, but I never expected it to come up this soon. Let's go!"

Christina couldn't resist. "Ok," she said. "But then we have to catch the bus and get back to the hotel. If Mimi gets worried, we'll be grounded for the whole trip and what fun would that be?"

Grant seemed to have forgotten all about Big Ben. The kids hurried across the street and toward the river.

But someone had overheard Grant and would not forget about him.

"How could such a little kid figure that out?" the dark, shaggy-headed man standing near the clock tower said to his friend.

"I don't know," said the man. He pulled an eraser from his backpack and scrubbed it over the

pencil sketch he had done earlier. "He's just a little kid with a big imagination. It was just a guess."

"Well, I guess we'd better keep an eye on him, anyway," said the first man. "C'mon." He stubbed out a smelly cigarette on the curb and started across the street to follow the excited children to the river.

The Eye in the Sky

"C'mon," said George. "Let's take this little snickleway." He pointed down a narrow alley. "It's a shortcut."

Christina giggled. She loved all the neat words she heard, even when she did not know what they meant half the time. She couldn't get over how old London was. The buildings all seemed to be like castles and palaces butted right next to modern skyscrapers. There were cathedrals and churches everywhere. Yummy-smells wafted from pubs, cafes, and restaurants.

After following Maggie and George down several twisted paths, the kids found themselves racing across a bridge over the Thames River (which Maggie and George pronounced TIMS) to the Eye Ferris wheel.

Christina and Grant loved to ride big rides, but this was a whopper and she could feel the butterflies leap in her stomach even before they boarded.

Maggie handed the ticket-taker their tickets and the kids climbed into the large glass-enclosed cars. At first, Christina thought that didn't seem like too much fun. She was used to Ferris wheels where you sat in cars with just a seat and sides and you could swing your feet in the air. But the Eye was so tall, she soon felt glad that it was enclosed.

At first she thought they would have the entire car to themselves, but at the last minute, two men shoved their way aboard. Both wore sloppy clothes and leather backpacks. Both had a snarl of dark, shaggy hair. But they stayed off to themselves even though it bothered Christina that they kept staring at the kids now and then.

"Wow, we are really up high!" said Grant as the wheel turned and propelled them up and up higher and higher over London.

"It doesn't move so fast, but it's the greatest view in the world!" said Maggie.

George had his face pressed against the glass.

They all looked out to see how far they could see. To Christina, London looked like a fairytale below as the night lights flickered on. The after-work traffic streamed across the bridges, leaving trails of red taillights from the cars and taxis and buses. In the distance, the sun seemed to sink all the way into tomorrow. Wait till she told Mimi and Papa about their ride! Uh, oh, she thought suddenly. It was almost dark. Mimi and Papa would not be happy if they did not get back to the hotel before dark.

"Aren't you having fun?" Maggie asked Christina.

Christina blushed. "Sure," she said, "but we need to get back soon, don't you think?"

Maggie shrugged her shoulders. "Yes, I guess so."

"Hey, look, there's Big Ben!" Grant cried.

Christina could not help but notice that the two men in their car really stared at Grant when he said that.

"And that's the end of our ride," said George, as they returned to the bottom of the circle and the door opened.

The kids scampered away from the Eye and followed Maggie to the taxi stand. "There's not much of a queue," she said. "Dad gave me taxi fare if we ever needed it," she told them. Then she said to Christina, "We'll get back to the hotel faster this way."

"Q?" said Grant. "What a q?"

"She means line, there's not much of a line," translated George.

And soon there was no line and the kids hustled into the waiting taxicab. As they drove off Christina noted that the two shaggy-headed, dark-skinned men had been in line behind them, but at the end of the queue, she was glad to see.

What she couldn't hear was one man say to the other, "Keep your eye on them. I have work to do, you know. And only 48 hours to get it done."

* * *

Just as the taxicab dropped them off in front of the hotel, dusk changed to just plain dark. The kids hurried inside, Christina sure they would be in trouble. But Mimi and Papa and Mr. Byron were still sitting in the Palm Court, much to her surprise. Mimi had changed into a long skirt with silver slippers and a shawl around her shoulders and the adults were laughing and sipping at their drinks and snacking on some dark stuff Christina thought might be caviar.

"Bonjour! Bonjour!" said Papa in welcome. You just never knew what language he would be speaking, no matter where he was. "What's up?"

"We rode the Eye!" Grant cried. "It was cool."

"And Gilbert looked out for you?" questioned Mr. Byron.

The kids looked at each other. "He looked out for us on the bus," said Maggie, "but we took a taxi back here."

The kids held their breath until Mimi said, "I'm so glad—I would have worried if you had not been here by dark."

The kids all sighed in relief. Adults were alike all around the world, Christina thought: Wash your hands before dinner. Do your homework. Be home by dark. Only with her grandparents, she and Grant always had one other rule: Don't get involved in mysteries. But maybe this time— as it often happened—it was already too late?

Jet Lag

The next morning was rainy. Christina was disappointed. She snuggled down in the "Princess and the Pea"—style bed and stared out the hotel window at the fat raindrops spattering the wavy glass.

Suddenly, the door to her room popped open and Papa grinned at her. "Only one good thing to do as a tourist on a rainy day, you know," he said.

"I know," said Christina, yawning. "Get thee to a museum." She had been on lots of trips with Mimi and Papa and could anticipate their answers to almost every dilemma.

"But not any old museum," Papa promised. "We're heading for the British Museum!" Papa tried to use his best English accent, but he still sounded like a cowboy to her.

Papa vanished just as quickly as he had appeared and Christina jumped up to dress. The British Museum was the oldest museum in the world. She just hoped Maggie and George were joining them, but it was not to be. They had school and Mimi was busy writing. So just she and Grant, who was already up and dressed, and Papa headed out for the museum adventure.

When they arrived at the museum and hopped out of the cab beneath Papa's enormous, gaudy (it looked like polka-dotted men's underwear) *brolly* (umbrella to she and Grant)— Christina was astounded. The Museum was just like something out of an old Indiana Jones movie. It was a huge stone building with large columns like some Greek temple.

"When I grow up, I'm going to be an explorer and bring good stuff back to gigantic museums like this," Grant said.

"Well, while you're growing, could you please move over and make room...I'm getting wet," grumbled Christina.

"Follow me!" said Papa, who never minded getting wet, as he strode right up to the entrance with his grandkids staggering to keep up beneath the big bright brolly.

Inside the museum, Christina felt as if she had entered a tomb. Everything was marble and tippy-toe quiet. Papa handed over their tickets and they headed directly for the Egyptian exhibit.

"Wow!" said Grant. "Look at all these mommies."

"Mummies, Grant," Christina corrected.

Grant stuck his arms out straight in front of him and staggered ahead with stiff legs. "Well some of these mummies must have been mommies. And this one—hey! This one is a cat!"

Christina giggled at the mummified cat. To her it looked sort of surprised, as if it did not really expect to run out of its "nine lives."

"Hey, Christina—walk like an Egyptian!" Grant changed his mummy walk into an Egyptian head-bobbing walk and Christina copied him.

"Ok, you guys, behave yourselves," said Papa.

"Tut-tut," said Grant in his own version of a British accent. "We shall." But he added in a tiny whisper only his sister heard. "Not!"

It was a morning filled with seeing new things. Papa showed them the Elgin Marbles, antiquities which had come from Greece. "The

Greeks want them back," Papa said.

"I can't blame them," said Christina, staring up at the beautiful marble scenes of men and horses.

"Uh, excuse me," said Grant. "Those men are uh, uh, nekkid."

Christina laughed. "Of course, they are, Grant. This is a museum. There are always lots of naked statues in museums."

Grant looked utterly confused. "And just why is that?" he asked.

Now it was Christina's turn to look puzzled. "Good question Grant; we'll have to ask Papa later." She said this because Papa had vanished around the corner. He liked to read everything while she and Grant liked to whisk from one thing to the other so they could see everything, which might take all day and all night in this place, she figured.

They were shocked to come around a corner and see a man who looked petrified. The information card said he was Lindow Man and was 2,000 years old.

"He looks it!" said Grant.

"It says the acid in a peat bog preserved him," Christina read.

"What's a peat bog?" asked Grant.

"I think it's dirt...like in a swamp or marsh," said Christina.

"Then let's stay away from those places," Grant said with a shiver. "Let's go find some people with clothes on, or at least skin."

That was fine with her, Christina thought. It seemed creepy and cold and dark and musty back in this part of the museum. No one else seemed to be around until Christina turned a corner and saw a piece of a person with dark hair scamper away behind a wall.

"Come on," Christina told her brother. "Let's go find the Rosetta Stone. That's where Papa said he was going."

The two kids wandered around the museum marveling at all the stuff there was to see. At last they came upon the exhibit housing the famous and historic Rosetta Stone.

"What is that thing?" Grant asked.

"It's a key to a code," Christina said, knowing Grant loved anything spylike, such as codes and ciphers.

"What code?" he asked, intrigued.

"Egyptian hieroglyphs," Christina explained.

"You mean those funky shapes that are

letters?" Grant said. Mimi had a necklace that made up the letters of her name—CAROLE—in hieroglyphs.

"That's right," Christina said, but Grant did not answer her. At first she could not find him and thought he had gone to look for Papa, but then she realized that he had crept beneath the Rosetta Stone and was picking up a piece of paper.

"Grant! Get out of there!" she said. "That thing is priceless, and if you break it I don't know how we pay for something that is *priceless*."

Grant wiggled out from under the stone and stood up. "If it's so valuable, people shouldn't put litter under it," he said. He held up the piece of paper for Christina to see. She took it from her brother and stared at it closely.

"Look, Grant!" she said. "It's a note or some kind of message—written in hieroglyphs!"

Grant looked at the writing. "I think I can figure this out," he said.

Even while Christina's stomach growled urgently for lunch, Grant insisted on working and working and working on the code. Soon, he had most of the letters figured out. "But I still don't get it," he said.

Christina took the note and read what he had filled in:

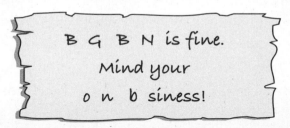

B G B N is fine.
Mind your
o n b siness!

Christina realized she could easily fill in the blanks now that Grant had done the hard part. "Grant, it says: BIG BEN is fine. Mind your own business!" Suddenly Christina realized that the note had been written with a faint pencil, almost like "henscratching," as Mimi would call it. It looked just like the pencil scrawl they had seen on the clock tower.

Grant look frightened. "Sounds like that piece of paper is not litter. Sounds like it was left there for us?"

Christina recalled seeing the snatch of dark unruly hair disappear around a corner earlier. "I think we're being followed," she whispered to her brother.

"I think we're being warned!" he whispered back.

Warned!

"Warned is right!" a deep voice behind them said. Christina and Grant jumped and turned. It was Papa.

"Did we do something wrong?" Christina asked.

"We didn't mean to," said Grant.

Papa gave a big sigh. "You disappeared from me in what seems like the largest museum in the world. I thought I'd never find you. Mimi would never forgive me if I lost you two, you know!"

The kids giggled. "But Papa," Christina said, "we always remember your rhyming rule: If the clock strikes 12, don't be a fool...always meet me in the vestibule."

Papa sighed again. "Well, I'm glad you remember my little rule that if we ever get separated to meet me by noon wherever we came in. But noon was one hour ago."

"Oh, wow!" said Christina. "We're sorry. I did not wear my watch and Grant and I got carried away trying to figure out...figure out..." Christina stopped. She did not think it was a good idea to tell about the note.

Thankfully, Grant came to her rescue. "Figure out the Rosetta Stone!"

At last, Papa took his hands off his hips and smiled. "Well, I'm glad you are that interested in history," he admitted. "But I plan to buy you both a watch at lunch so this won't happen again."

"I'm sure ready for lunch," Christina said, rubbing her middle, "but where are we going that we can get lunch *and* a watch?"

Papa raised his thick black eyebrows high. "And a wedding dress, or a very large salmon, or a diamond ring, or a tremendous teddy bear, or..."

Christina interrupted her grandfather. "Where is *that*?!"

"You'll see," said Papa, secretively. "Follow me."

* * *

The three tourists sped through the rain in another taxicab through busy London streets. At last they stopped in front of a large department store: HARROD'S the sign read.

"Wait till you see this place!" Papa said. "Mimi is meeting us here for lunch. She has to buy a hat to wear to meet the Queen."

"Mimi never needs an excuse that big to buy a hat," Christina said with a giggle.

"*Shopping*," said Grant in a bored voice. "I'd rather be back with the mummies."

But once in the store, he changed his mind. Harrod's was beautiful. It was big. It smelled of good things like perfume and chocolate. It was bright. And busy. And best of all, tagging along with Mimi were Maggie and George.

"Hi!" the kids all yelled at one another and hugged.

"We got to get out of school early," said Maggie.

"We got to get out of trouble," said Grant.

"Trouble?" said Mimi. "I don't like the sound of that." She frowned at Papa.

"Just kidding, Mimi," Grant said instantly, but

his grandmother still looked suspicious.

Papa herded them all toward Harrod's famous food court, but it was not like any food court Christina had ever seen. It was majestic hall after hall of fish market, and baked goods, and candy, and cheese, and tea, and gifts, and soda fountain. Papa picked each child up in turn and sat them on a tall stool at the soda fountain. "You get to eat here," he said. "And Mimi and I will be right over there." He pointed to a smaller marble counter that had soup and salads and champagne.

"This is great!" said Christina after her grandparents walked off. "I'm starving."

"Yeah," said Grant. "Mystery always makes me hungry, too."

"Mystery?" said George.

"Mystery?" said Maggie. "I thought you guys just went to the museum. What was so mysterious there?"

After they ordered chili dogs and milkshakes, Christina pulled the note out of her pocket and spread it on the counter. "Remember the sketch and the guys at Big Ben yesterday?" she said.

Maggie looked shocked. "Oh, no," she said. "We forgot all about that."

George thought his sister was serious. "Of course we remember that, and being followed too. Did you see those guys again?"

"Shhh!" warned Christina. "I'm not sure. We saw somebody or part of somebody. But Grant found this note written in hieroglyphs and translated most of it. When I filled in the blanks, this is what it said." She pointed to the message and Maggie and George read it silently.

"Wow," said Maggie. "That sounds like a warning?"

"But about what?" asked Christina, frustrated. "We're just a bunch of kids. Sure, we saw that scrawling on Big Ben, but big deal. What do they think we are going to do?"

Grant seemed very serious. He stirred his milkshake instead of drinking it. "Maybe it is a big deal," he said. "Maybe there really is a bomb and they really are going to blow up Big Ben."

George chimed in. "Maybe we are just kids but those guys took the trouble to follow you and at least warn us to stay out of the way."

"So what should we do?" Maggie asked.

Christina groaned. "I know what we should do," she said. "But do we really want to?"

Maggie and George looked puzzled, but

Grant didn't.

"Tell Mimi and Papa?" he guessed.

"And spoil a good mystery?" Christina said.

"But what if Big Ben really is in trouble?" said Grant.

"What if we really are in big trouble?" said Maggie.

"Like what?" asked George.

"Like the bad guys don't leave us alone," said Maggie.

Teddy Bears and Tooth Brushes

The kids had a chance to forget about their troubles for a while. After lunch, they tagged along with Mimi to the haberdashery department and critiqued her choices:

"Too big!"

"Too small?"

"Too frou-frou."

"Too bloody awful!!" (That was Papa's comment about the pink and purple paisley chapeau.)

Exasperated, Mimi finally shooed them all away and they headed for the incredible Harrod's toy department. The boys rushed off to see the train displays. The girls made a beeline for the dolls.

"Gee," said Christina, "what a great place. You could get everything you want for Christmas right here!" She thought she had never seen so much of everything "toy" in one place. It was so overwhelming in fact that she could only think of one thing to buy. "I think I will get a Harrod's teddy bear for my cousin Avery," she said. Avery would be almost three at Christmas and Christina felt sure she would love a big, fat-bellied bear to sleep with in the new room she was going to move into before her new baby brother or sister was born.

As Christina stepped into the queue for the cash register, a swarthy man in baggy pants with shaggy hair rushed up to her. He looked just about as out of place among the Barbie dolls and girly toys as the Easter Bunny in a Santa suit.

Christina gasped. The man stuck his face right into hers and shook his finger. "YOU HAVE BEEN WARNED!" he hissed.

Christina cringed. Maggie screamed. Then Christina did something she had never expected to do: She hollered at the top of her lungs—"FIRE!"

Scotland Yard

That night back at the Ritz, the adults and kids had a meeting around a large, dark oak table like something out of King Arthur and the Knights of the Roundtable.

The adults sat in big, high-backed chairs. So did the kids, only they looked—and felt—very small and afraid, especially since the only person standing—a very serious man from Scotland Yard (the London police department) looked down at them as if they were very squashable bugs.

"Ahem," he said. "Let me go over this thing one more time." He tapped his pencil on his notepad. Grant groaned under his breath. They had been "over this thing" about 40 times, it seemed. Mimi gave Grant "the look" that meant "behave yourself or else."

The detective continued. "You saw something at Big Ben. You found a note at the museum. You had a shaggy-haired guy yell at you in Harrod's...and you screamed 'Fire!'—right?"

Christina felt like she could bawl. "Yes," she admitted, for the umpteenth time. "Papa always said that when we were in danger we should yell fire, instead of help—that people would pay more attention."

People had paid attention all right. When Christina had cried out, the man had dashed away. Fire alarms started screeching so loudly that you could not think. Harrod's had been evacuated, and it was only because no smoke was detected that the sprinkler system had not gone off and turned the toy department into a lake.

The worse thing was that the man had escaped and Christina had lost the note in the shuffle, and so the kids had no evidence to prove what they were claiming. The police had been to Big Ben and found no sign of the sketch on the side of the clock tower.

Mimi came to the kids' defense. "I have never known these children to tell a lie," she asserted. "While you may have no proof as to what they say, you certainly have no proof that they are making things up."

Papa agreed. "I can assure you that we will keep a tight rein on these children. But I suggest you focus on your job and let us focus on ours."

Mr. Byron was there, too. He seemed quite embarrassed by the entire situation. What if the newspapers picked up this news? Surely it would be embarrassing for his publishing company and perhaps reflect negatively on Mimi and her forthcoming book?

The detective cleared his throat. He seemed to have come to a decision. "We will continue to investigate," he said. "And YOU," he said, pointing to the children, "continue to be good little tourists and school students. Leave the mysteries to solve to me."

"And me," Mimi said under her breath. Christina could not help herself; she giggled. The detective glared at her.

"We don't take the word 'bombing' lightly in London these days," he said to Christina. "I suggest you not use that word again." The kids could tell it was not a suggestion—it was an ORDER!

The man from Scotland Yard left and

everyone relaxed.

"I think he thinks he's Sherlock Holmes," said George, referring to the famous fictional London detective from author Sir Arthur Conan Doyle's crime novels.

"I think he thinks we're Jack the Ripper," said Maggie. She meant the really bad meanie who once killed women around London in a very nasty way.

Papa stood up. "I think he means business...and so do I. You know what happens to kids who do not obey their parents and grandparents?"

"What?" asked Grant in a tiny voice.

Papa winked at Mr. Byron who bellowed: "We send them to the Tower of London!"

"What's that?" Grant asked.

"Tomorrow's Saturday," said Maggie. "We'll show you."

As the kids got up and headed out of the room behind the men, Christina noticed Mimi sitting silently at the table. She could tell her grandmother's little gray mystery brain cells were working overtime. What she could not tell was that Mimi was truly worried. She really did know that her imaginative grandchildren knew fact from fiction and had the same instincts for mystery that she had. If they had seen or felt or heard something was amiss...well, it probably was. She would have to keep a very good eye on them. And knowing Grant and Christina, she knew that they would not like that at all.

The Infamous Tower of London

The next morning was bright and sunny. Everyone was in a much better mood. The newspapers had run only a small story about the "false alarm" at Harrod's the previous day. There was no mention of shaggy-headed men or kids or anything about bombs. Christina felt sure that the man from Scotland Yard had something to do with that.

After a full English breakfast of bacon, eggs, tomatoes, sausage, and fried bread, the kids had met at Tower Bridge. Fortunately, the kids were pretty much left to enjoy themselves, while Mr. Byron followed behind at a discrete distance. He was their chaperone (or babysitter) for the day while Mimi and Papa worked on "the book" and getting ready to visit the Queen.

"So this is London Bridge?" asked Grant. He put his hands on his hips and bent backwards to stare up at the two twin towers of the tall bridge that spanned the Thames River.

"No," Maggie corrected him. "London Bridge is in Arizona."

"Huh?" said Christina. "Arizona is in America."

"We know where Arizona is," Maggie said, smugly. "A few years ago, someone in America bought our London Bridge and took it down and moved it to Arizona. This is Tower Bridge."

"Hey!" said Grant. "Whatever bridge it is, it's a drawbridge!" The kids watched as the center of the large bridge split in two, each section rising up into the sky to allow a large ship to pass.

When it finally closed back down, the kids scampered on across the bridge, Mr. Byron following, working a crossword puzzle as he walked.

"So this is the Tower of London?" Christina asked, as they approached the tall white towers on the other side of the river. "What happened here?"

George just snickered ominously. "What *didn't* happen here is what you should ask!"

Christina had learned by now that when the English said "tower" or "cathedral" or "park" or "palace" that they did not really mean one single place but an entire complex of things. Tower of London was no exception. There seemed to be a multitude of towers, enclosed spaces, and, as she soon learned, plenty of underground dungeons.

Grant spotted a man wearing a black outfit with red embroidery on it and a tall black hat. "Is he Scotland Yard?" he asked, suspiciously.

"No," said George. "He is a Beefeater."

"Well, so am I," said Grant. "I eat hamburgers all the time."

"No, Grant," said Maggie. "A Beefeater is one of the 42 yeomen who guard the tower."

"Well, why didn't you say so?" said Grant, indignantly.

"I did!" spouted George.

Christina laughed. "I can see we speak the same English, only not really. Forget about it, Grant, and ask why the Tower of London is supposed to be so spooky. I don't see anything that bothers me."

Maggie and George just exchanged "looks" and snickered.

At first, the Tower still seemed rather innocent to Christina. They went inside and waded along with the other tourists past the Crown Jewels. These were an incredible display of crowns, scepters, orbs, swords, and other paraphernalia related to the coronation of England's many kings and queens.

"Uh, I think that's a pretty big diamond," Christina said, marveling at the enormous glittering jewel in one crown.

"Uh, yeah!" said Maggie. "Like more than 500 carets."

"That diamond is not made of carrots!" argued Grant. "It isn't even orange."

Maggie laughed, but Christina put her arm around Grant to comfort him. "That's how they measure the size of a diamond," she told her brother. "It's carets, not carrots. And you only learn by asking," she said, mainly to Maggie.

"That's true," Maggie agreed. "I guess if I came to America there would be a lot that I don't know."

Christina nodded at her agreeably. Grant and George had already scampered off to see the historic display of weapons such as guns and swords. But all the kids grew quiet as they came to the displays of armor. Christina had forgotten that "knights in shining armor" were not just the stuff of fairytales. The shiny silver scales that made up a suit of armor made her think of the armadillos they often saw stiff and dead on the side of the highway back home.

"How did they go to the bathroom?" was what Grant wanted to know, but neither Maggie nor George had an answer for that one.

Neither Grant nor Christina could believe the next part of the Tower tour. They both cringed at the stories the tour guide told of torture in the Tower. They were appalled at the "rack" where prisoners were stretched until their bones broke, in an effort to make them to confess to deeds, whether they had committed them or not.

The "scavenger's daughter" was another Dark Ages device, used to squash the body—and the prisoner—into confessions.

Maggie told them how many people had been beheaded on the guillotine, having their head chopped off by a sharp falling blade. And then there was the story of two boy princes, thrown into the dungeon, never to be seen again—so someone else could come into power.

"You do have a bloody history," Christina criticized.

"Well, you killed the Indians," Maggie retorted.

Christina was silent. She thought bad things were bad things, no matter which country or which period of time. "I get the picture!" Christina said. "Now can't we go see something more cheerful?"

Somehow, during the tour, they had lost Mr. Byron. Christina thought she would have been glad to see his face and to have a nice grandfather lead them back out into the sunshine and to some place warm and pleasant with ice cream for sale.

Maggie nodded and turned and began to lead the children back up the stairs, but when they arrived at an entranceway leading outdoors, Christina turned to find that Grant had...

Vanished!

Skip to M'loo, My Darlin'

Christina was relieved and surprised to find Grant sitting on a bench with Mr. Byron. Grant was helping him with answers to the crossword puzzle Mr. Byron was working.

"Did you enjoy your tour?" Mr. Byron asked. He stretched and stood up. "Would you like to get some ice cream?"

The kids cheered. Mr. Byron led the way and Grant bowed and let the girls go first.

"How chivalrous!" Maggie complimented Grant.

"Well, I was cold," Grant said, misunderstanding the word, "but it's warmer outside of that dank, dark dungeon."

"She means you're polite," said Christina,

looking back over her shoulder. "Like knights of yore..." But now Grant really had vanished. Why couldn't her little brother ever keep up, she wondered. She figured he had run on ahead or taken a shortcut to be first in the ice cream line. But when the girls caught up with Mr. Byron, Grant was nowhere to be seen.

"Where's your brother?" George asked Christina.

Christina was not worried and she didn't want Grant to get in trouble, so she said, "Oh, I'll bet he went to the restroom, or something."

"The loo," Maggie corrected her. "We say the loo."

Suddenly, Grant appeared from around a corner. "Well, skip to the loo, my darlin's," he chirped. "I think you'd better come with me," he whispered behind his hand to Christina.

"Can we walk around and make some snapshots?" Christina asked Mr. Byron quickly.

"Every tourist does," he said, heading for the nearest bench to resume his crossword puzzle.

"What's up?" Christina and Maggie asked, as soon as Mr. Byron was out of earshot.

Grant did not answer. Instead, he led them a ways down a path toward the river. "Look," he finally said. "See the towers of the Tower of London...and those of Tower Bridge? You can climb up there—there are steps inside; I see them."

"So?" said George.

"So," said Grant, "Maybe you can get up inside the clock tower at Big Ben. Maybe someone can really get up there and plant a bomb, that they can make go off by remote control."

Maggie shook her head. "I don't think so. You're not allowed."

Christina laughed mockingly. "Well, terrorists don't usually stand around obeying orders and following rules." When she saw Mr. Byron watching them suspiciously, she began to make pictures with her camera, just pointing and aiming at anything, not even looking through the viewfinder.

"But why would anyone blow up Big Ben anyway?" George asked. "Everybody loves Big Ben."

"Sometimes people just want to cause turmoil," Christina said. "They want to attack or destroy things people love or are proud of."

"Like the Statue of Liberty in your country?" guessed Maggie. "Yes," said

Christina. "Like Big Ben in yours...something that stands for national pride."

"But why do people want to do such dastardly deeds?" Grant asked. Christina knew he must have picked up that phrase from some of the mystery and detective books he loved to read.

"Just mean and mixed up, Mimi says," said Christina, shrugging her shoulders.

Maggie plopped down on the grass and the others joined her. She began to pick wild daisies and chain them together. "Well we're not supposed to be thinking about Big Ben," she reminded them.

"And certainly not *doing* anything about Big Ben," added Christina.

Grant was very quiet. He continued to stare at the towers. Christina could see the wheels turning in his head, just like the drawbridge wheels turning in the towers. She knew he would not give up worrying about Big Ben and she really didn't know whether to encourage or discourage her brother regarding the matter.

Then Grant did something that helped them all make a decision...he opened his hand.

Showing Your Hand

"What's that?" asked George. He looked down at the sketch scrawled in ink on the palm of Grant's hand.

"It's how I think the bad guys would do it," said Grant. "See: here is the clock tower, the stairs, the top. It would be easy to get up there and plant a bomb and set the wires or timer—or whatever you do—and then escape and set it off from a distance with a cell phone or something. Then KABOOM!"

No one liked the sound of that. But no one said a word.

Finally, Christina said, "Well, what do you suggest we do?"

"Go up and see!" said Grant.

"I have a better idea," said George. The kids just stared at him, so he continued. "Since the bad guys were following us, why don't we follow them...and see what they're up to."

Maggie looked aggravated. "Because we don't know where they are," she said, having to hold her tongue and not add "stupid."

George just smiled at them. "We just might have a chance to find out where they are."

"How?" Grant asked eagerly.

George nodded back toward his grandfather, still sitting on the bench. "Granddad has a visitor."

The children spun around on the grass and saw the Scotland Yard detective standing over Mr. Byron. They were talking animatedly. The detective was waving a piece of paper around.

Without a word, the kids slowly sidled up and sat on a bench behind the adults. They pretended that they were not paying a bit of attention to them, but in fact, they were eavesdropping so hard their ears hurt.

"We've heard the Globe... Piccadilly Circus... Madame Tussaud's, Cleopatra's Needle, St. Paul's Cathedral, even the Palace," they overheard him say. He waved a piece of paper in the air. "Are you certain that the children cannot tell us anything else?"

Christina noticed a bulge beneath the detective's

coat; she figured it was a gun. Mr. Byron held his hand above his eyes, shielding them from the bright sun. He could not see the kids. Indeed, he must have felt like he was under interrogation. The detective sounded desperate and determined.

"I am certain the kids do not know anything else," Mr. Byron assured the detective. He sounded just as determined.

At last the detective shook his head and then shook hands with Mr. Byron. "Please call the Yard if you think of anything," he said dejectedly. He turned on his heels, spraying blades of grass, and stalked off, wadding his list into a ball and tossing it down on the ground in disgust.

Mr. Byron looked out across the lawn for the kids. He could not spot them because they were behind the bench. Beneath the bench was the piece of paper the detective had discarded. Christina put her finger to her lips and indicated SHHH! Then she snaked her arm beneath the bench and picked up the note right by Maggie's and George's granddad's foot!

* * *

Later that night, back at the hotel, the kids had no way to communicate with one another except via

instant messaging on the computer. Christina began.
Maggie, can we get together early tomorrow?

Christina, sure; we are out of school. Granddad said
we could ride the bus again with cousin Gilbert!

Oh, boy, that's a stroke of good luck.

What do you think we should do?

Trust Grant's instincts. We don't want anything to
happen to Big Ben. We sure don't want anything to be
bombed.

But, it's dangerous!

I know. I know. See you tomorrow.

Later that night, Christina transferred the
pictures from her digital camera to her computer.
The very first shot showed parts of two men—both
with shaggy brown hair, both with bulges under their
jackets, but both from the back so she could not see
their faces. To keep the fear factor down, she decided
not to tell the others.

Piccadilly Circus

The next day proved to be one of the busiest Christina had ever known. Maggie and George showed up early, holding big red bus passes for four. Grant had the "list." Christina had her camera. George had an iPod filled with Beatles music which he listened to and danced to, looking silly since no one else could hear the music.

Mimi (who had to write) and Papa (who had to run meet-the-Queen errands) had given them "the lecture" about behaving and staying out of trouble. Mr. Byron had to attend an editorial meeting. When they boarded the first bus, cousin Gilbert just waved. The kids waved back and sat on the upper deck as far away from Gilbert as possible, but it was not necessary—he was clearly keeping his eye on girls, not kids.

Christina thought it was great fun to ride so high up and see all the sights. London was busy this morning. People were heading to work, tourists were everywhere, kids were on school holiday so they were out and about too. Traffic was snarled. Horns blared. Sirens screeched. It was the big city bustle that Christina and Mimi loved.

"First stop: Piccadilly Circus!" shouted Grant, spotting a sign. The kids scampered down the staircase and off the back of the bus. Gilbert never even looked.

The kids had decided that the detective's list suggested other possibilities for disaster. They thought that if they could visit each place, then they might eliminate Big Ben from the "hit list"...and maybe even spy the bad guys somewhere—even though Christina was not too thrilled about that idea.

As soon as they hit the sidewalk, Grant spun round and round. "Ok, where is it? Where's the circus?" he asked.

Maggie and George laughed. "This IS the Circus!" they said in unison.

Grant and Christina looked equally puzzled.

"Then where is the big top tent?" asked

Grant. "And the elephants and the clowns?"

"And the cotton candy?" Christina joined in.

Maggie and George just sighed as if they had explained all this before to former tourist visitors.

"Piccadilly Circus is just a place..." Maggie began.

"...where you come to head for the cinemas or theaters," finished George. "Sort of like your Times Square in New York City."

Grant just shrugged in disappointment.

"Well, we might as well look around," said Christina, waving her arm at the endless array of enormous neon advertising signs. "This would be a good place to set off a bomb if you were a terrorist, I guess. I mean there are lots and lots of people around."

"No!" Grant argued. "It's Big Ben."

"We could stand here all day," Maggie said, or we could move on to the next place?"

"Hey, who's that dude?" Grant interrupted. The others thought he might have spied one of the bad guys and turned this way and that, looking all around.

Finally, Maggie realized that Grant meant the statue nearby. "That's Eros," she said, "the

Greek god of love. You know—from mythology."

"Oh, barf bags!" said Grant, grabbing his waist and bending over. "He'd better keep that Cupid's arrow away from us, right George?"

George blushed.

"Don't ask George—he has a girlfriend!" Maggie told on her brother. "Ophelia."

Grant looked stunned. "OH FEEL YA?" he said.

Christina giggled. "Grant, it's an English name," she explained, but Grant just paraded off to the bus stop without them and they had to hurry up to catch the bus to St. Paul's Cathedral. In their rush, they failed to see the two men crammed into one of London's bright red phone booths pretending to make a phone call.

* * *

Now it was Christina's turn to be astounded. "Wow! What a church!" she said, as she put her hands on her waist and bent back to stare up at the beautiful St. Paul's Cathedral. "This is what Mimi would call an edifice."

"This is one of London's main tourist attractions," Maggie explained. "The cathedral is famous. It was designed by the famous architect Christopher Wren. It was destroyed during the 1666 Great Fire of London. And in World War II, men and boys threw buckets of water on the dome to keep it from burning from the bombs that German airplanes were dropping on it."

"Bombs, bombs, bombs," Grant grumbled. "I never heard so much about bombs since the World Trade Centers attacks."

Christina put her arm around her little brother. "Don't be discouraged, Grant," she said. "There have always been bad guys, but they never win out in the end. This cathedral is proof!"

The gigantic building with its dome and towers was very impressive. But it was even more impressive inside in the beautiful sanctuary.

"It has flying buttresses," said George as they all stood beneath the grand dome and looked up so far that it made them dizzy.

"Flying *what*?" Grant asked, but George ignored him.

"Come on!" George said, instead. "We'll show you our favorite place—the Whispering Gallery." Maggie nodded eagerly.

Grant and Christina had to scamper along behind their friends at a rapid pace to keep up. Soon they were indeed going UP: up and up endless circular stairs until they finally reached a balcony high up in the dome.

"Wow!" Christina said. "This is a great view."

"True," said Maggie, "but what's famous about this gallery is the acoustics—you can whisper and hear one another from anywhere along the balcony." To prove her point, she headed for the far side of the gallery.

Grant and George moved away as well and Christina stayed where she was. When everyone was in position, Maggie whispered, "Can you hear me?"

Christina giggled. She could indeed hear Maggie from way across the expanse of open dome. Maggie giggled because she could hear Christina giggle. Then they both stopped abruptly when some adults gave them a mean "this is a church, you know" look.

Next, Grant piped up. "Do you see what I see?" he asked so loudly that there were more mean looks from the other tourists.

"Grant, whisper," Christina begged.

"But look!" Grant said, not quite as loud. The

other kids stared down over the balcony onto the floor of the cathedral.

"What?" whispered Christina.

"SHH!" said a tourist.

"Where?" whispered George.

"SHHH!" said a different tourist.

"Who?" whispered Maggie.

"SHHHHHHHH!" said three tourists.

Quickly, the kids looked where Grant pointed. Two dark, bushy headed men with backpacks stood near a column down on the cathedral floor. They seemed to be looking at a note.

Just as quickly, the four children scampered back down the spiraling staircase. But by the time they reached the bottom, the men had disappeared. However, at the bottom of the column was a folded piece of paper. Grant ran over and picked it up. It was just an informational brochure about St. Paul's.

Grant hastily scanned the smooth white column to see if any sketch had been drawn on it. He found nothing.

"What do we do now?" asked Christina.

"Pray?" asked Maggie.

Cleopatra's Needle

The kids stood back outside in the sunshine. The presumed "bad guys" were nowhere to be seen.

"Of course, looking for them in St. Paul's is like looking for a needle in a haystack," George grumbled.

"Hey! I forgot—Cleopatra's Needle was one place on the detective's list," Maggie reminded them. "If we catch this bus we can get there."

"No," George disagreed. "We'll have to change buses. Let's take the tube; it's faster."

"The tube?" said Grant, hopefully. "Is it a water park tube? A theme park ride?"

Maggie laughed. "No, Grant, we mean the

London Underground—what you call the subway in New York City."

"Well, that's cool, too," Grant said. "Let's go!"

Maggie quickly checked a list of Underground routes posted nearby. "We can take the Circle," she said. "Follow me!"

And before the others could object, Maggie sped off. The rest of the kids followed her down some stairs by a red and blue circular Underground sign. Maggie bought tickets from an automatic machine and the others copied her by feeding their tickets into another machine which admitted them to a platform.

Christina laughed out loud. It was such a zoo! People were scrambling everywhere. And everyone seemed to know where they were going except her. She just hoped Maggie knew what she was doing.

"What does MIND THE GAP mean?" Grant asked, as Christina grabbed him by the back of his tee shirt before he fell into an opening to the train tracks between the platform and the trains.

Maggie and George laughed. "THAT'S what it means!" George said. "Watch out or you'll end up under the train instead of on it."

Christina shuddered and held Grant's

hand, even though he squirmed like mad, until the train that was coming their way stopped and the doors *swished* open and the kids clambered aboard.

It seemed like before they could sit down or get comfortable, that Maggie was squealing, "Get off here!" and the kids tumbled out of the train—minding the gap—and onto another platform. Up the steps she sped, the others racing to keep up.

As the four kids spewed out of the Underground station, the bright sunlight temporarily blinded them.

"I see them!" George screamed, racing ahead.

"I can't see anything," Christina complained, shielding her eyes from the sun with her hand.

"Me neither," said Maggie.

"It isn't them," said Grant, pointing to two boys up ahead. "False alarm."

George was aggravated. "How do you know?" he asked grumpily. "Just because you didn't see them first?"

"No," Grant promised, sticking his Boy Scout fingers up. "I could just tell."

"Wow," said Christina. "Look around. When you actually start looking, there are lots and lots of tall guys in dark clothes with long, dark hair wearing backpacks. I guess they're all students?"

"Probably," said Maggie. "That's the way Gilbert always dresses when he is in school and not driving the bus."

"We're not looking for students," Grant groused. "We're looking for terrorists, and I'll know them when I see them."

Dispirited, the kids trudged toward the monument they were seeking—Cleopatra's Needle. When they came upon it, Christina was enthralled, as she always was with anything Egyptian. The tall, pink, stone obelisk looked very old. In fact, the plaque nearby said that it was much older than the city of London—erected in 1500 BCE.

"Can you read hieroglyphs?" George asked Christina.

"No, but Grant can," Christina answered.

"Really?" asked Maggie, in disbelief.

Grant shrugged his shoulders. "Sure," he said, as if it were easy and every kid could read the ancient Egyptian writing. He stared at all the mysterious, faded markings. Then he shook his head forlornly.

"Ohh," said George, misinterpreting Grant's somber look.

"Does it say something awful?"

Grant pursed his lips together and nodded his head slowly up and down.

"Terrifying?" asked Maggie, her voice almost trembling.

"Really?" asked Christina, not fooled by her brother's play-acting.

"IT SAYS I'M STARVING!" Grant hollered out. "And I can't solve any mystery when my tummy is rumbling louder than a mummy."

"Mummies don't talk," George argued, not appreciating Grant's shenanigans.

Grant looked thoughtful, then said, "They do if you cut a teeny, tiny slit in their dry cleaning." He put two fingers like scissors to his lips and pretended to snip.

"Oh, Grant," said Maggie. "You are too silly. I agree. Let's pop in this pub for a bite and maybe we can think straighter."

* * *

In the dark pub, the kids pulled heavy chairs up to a large round table. A waitress in a jester-type outfit took their order and soon they were munching on hot fish with lemony tarter sauce.

"I thought we were getting chips," said Grant.

"Those are chips," George said, pointing to Grant's plate. "We all have them."

"Those are French fries," Grant argued, popping one, dripping ketchup, into his mouth.

Maggie laughed. "You call them fries; we call them chips." Christina wiped her mouth of root beer foam. "Communication—maybe that's what this is all about."

"What do you mean?" asked Maggie.

Christina looked thoughtful. "I think I mean that we are running around on a wild goose chase. We just don't have enough information. We are just guessing. We really need another clue to help us along."

"Well I don't have a clue as to how to get another clue," said Grant, grumpily.

Maggie nodded sympathetically. "The only thing we have to go on right now is the detective's list. But there are still some places that we have not visited. Perhaps we should just stick to our knitting and see where that gets us. What choice do we have?"

The others agreed and finished their lunch so

they could head back out, when Maggie said. "I'll be just a minute. I need to spend a penny." She hopped up and left the table.

Grant watched her go as if she were crazy. "What is she going to spend a penny on?"

George giggled. "That's just an expression. She meant she had to go to the bathroom, the loo."

Grant shook his head. "Then why didn't she just say so?"

Christina giggled. "She did!" she told her brother, then muttered to herself... *communication, indeed!*

To Be or Not to Be

Back outside, the kids decided to take a ride up the Thames River to the Globe Theater, one of the places on the detective's list.

"The Globe Theater seems like an odd place to be on the list of possible places to bomb," said Christina, as they stood in the ticket queue.

"Yes," George agreed. "What does it have in common with Big Ben, St. Paul's, and places like that?"

"I guess it's just another famous London area location that would make headlines if it were bombed," Maggie guessed.

"It should make WORLD headlines!" Grant said, as he twirled 'round and 'round a sign pole.

"And why is that, Grant?" asked Christina. She just knew her brother would have some silly comeuppance answer, and he did.

"Because ALL THE WORLD'S A STAGE!" he intoned in a deep, actor's voice, quoting Shakespeare. He was disappointed when the other kids did not fall over laughing. Instead, they wore serious frowns on their faces.

"You could be sadly right," Maggie moaned, then added, "Come on! The boat is here."

The children scampered aboard the flat-bottomed boat for their tour up the Thames River. Grant and Christina had grown up around boats and loved being on the water. Mimi and Papa often took them to Bath, North Carolina (named after Bath, England) to ride the ferry boats that ran between the Outer Banks. That was where Blackbeard, known as the fiercest pirate of them all, had come to from England. They also boated on the Intracoastal Waterway around Savannah, Georgia.

"This is so much fun," Christina said. She liked that there was so much to look at on each side of the river. She wished a big river ran through their town back home. She could just imagine "Merrie Olde England" back when it was a new, bustling port town. Perhaps Sir Walter Raleigh had sailed to America from these very waters. Oops, she thought, remembering her fourth-grade social studies—Sir Walter Raleigh never came to the New World!

"Maybe we could pop in the water for a swim?" suggested Grant, beginning to cobble together some typical English phrases.

"EWWW!" whined Maggie and George together. "And maybe you could die of plague," George added.

"You mean the water's that polluted?" Christina asked, astounded. She hated pollution and litter—they were her two pet peeves.

"The Black Death once killed thousands in London," Maggie reminded them.

"Rats spread the plague," George said, cringing.

Christina shivered. She HATED anything creepy-crawly; she couldn't help it. But RATS, they were the worst. "I avoid rats like the plague!" she swore to the others.

"Have you ever actually seen a rat?" George asked.

Christina thought hard. "Well maybe only a mouse, but that's close enough for me."

"You wanna see a wharf rat?" George asked mischievously.

"I do!" Grant cried eagerly.

"Then just look right over there!" George said, pointing toward the thick lines tied between a battered old wharf and the rusty hulk of an abandoned ship.

Everyone turned to look, and sure enough, a large wharf rat was climbing up the rope like an acrobat. He dripped water from his hair and long tail, and seemed to stop to stare back at them before he vanished into the ship's scupper.

"Yikes!" cried Christina. "I'm not getting on that boat." Then she began to hop on one foot and then the other, looking around beneath her seat, and satisfied that there was nothing more there than some leftover candy bar papers, shoved her feet beneath her on the seat...just to be safe.

The others laughed. "Don't be a scaredy cat," George said.

"I'd be a scaredy cat of a rat that big even if I were a big rat-eating cat," Christina admitted and the kids laughed again.

Then the foursome settled down to admire the more pleasant scenery along the way: lovely riverside gardens, quaint pubs with funny names like Ye Olde Eel House, castle spires, Roman-era walls, and much more.

Soon the boatman called, "The Globe!" and the kids stamped down the gangplank to the dock. Christina surreptitiously took a peek to make sure there were no rats running around beneath her feet.

Maggie was back in her tour guide mode. "William Shakespeare is the world's most famous playwright. He not only wrote famous plays like *Romeo and Juliet* and *Macbeth*, he acted in plays too. He had a large family. The Globe was one of the theaters where his plays were performed. Sometimes rich people sent their servants to stand in line to buy tickets for them. If you paid a certain price, you could sit close to the stage and even tease the actors or tickle them with straw. Women weren't allowed to be actors, so men had to play the parts of women characters, too."

"Not me!" swore Grant. "Methinks no, no, no."

"Well, now that we're here, what do we look for?" asked Christina.

"Anything suspicious," suggested George.

"Anything that looks like that!" Grant

insisted. And, sure enough, he pointed to two men with backpacks, reading a posted notice of an audition. Long, scraggy hair hung down over their backpacks.

Quietly, the kids sneaked closer and closer until they were right behind the suspicious-looking characters. Suddenly, the two men turned and screamed at the kids, "GETTETH AWAY FROM US!" The four children screamed at the top of their lungs and ran as far and as fast as they could back to the boat landing.

221b Baker Street

Once back on board their boat for the return trip to London, Christina asked her brother, "Do you think that was them? Do you think those were the guys we saw at Big Ben?"

Grant was jammed into a corner seat, his knees tucked up under his arms. His hair was sweaty from running so fast and stood straight up where he had swiped it with the palm of his hand.

"I don't know," he said. "I'm not sure. All these guys seem to look alike. How can we tell one shaggy-headed, bearded guy from another, especially if they all wear grungy clothes and beat-up, old backpacks?"

"Good question," said George. "Perhaps we should stop here for some help?"

The kids looked to see that George indicated the stop coming up. A notice board listed the nearby attractions. One of them was 221b Baker Street—home of famous fictional detective Sherlock Holmes.

Without a word, the kids hopped off the boat when it stopped. Maggie led the way. It seemed she had been to every place in London on either school field trips or Saturday holiday outings with her family.

"So we think Mr. Holmes will help us solve our mystery?" Grant asked as they approached the building.

The others laughed. "What's so funny?" demanded Grant.

"Sherlock Holmes isn't real," Christina reminded him. "He's a fictional detective created by Sir Arthur Conan Doyle."

"But I've seen him in the old movies Mimi likes to watch," argued Grant. "He wears that funky hat and cape and smokes a big ol' pipe."

"That's called a deerstalker hat," said Maggie, meaning a hat with flaps on both sides tied up on top and a bill on both the front and the back. "That was just an actor playing the detective."

"Well that makes him a defective detective in my book if he's not even real," Grant said.

Christina thought how it was often difficult to sort out fact from fiction. Maybe this whole idea of a couple of terrorist-type thugs trying to blow up Big Ben was really just their imagination carried away with red herrings. She figured she'd better not mention red herrings to Grant or he would be looking all around for fish instead of false clues to a mystery that possibly didn't exist. Now she had confused herself, she thought. How does Mimi keep mysteries straight when she writes, she wondered.

Just then the door to 221b Baker Street burst open and Sherlock Holmes' housekeeper (or the person hired to pretend to be her) beckoned them in to the detective's rooms.

The kids looked and listened and eventually wandered up a lot of stairs to the fourth floor where Christina bought Mimi a bright yellow deerslayer hat just for fun.

When they were back outside, Grant said, "Well, did that help us any?"

"It made me want to read some Sherlock Holmes' stories," said George.

"It made me hungry and tired," said Grant.

"We've been gone all day. Can't we go home now?"

Christina looked around. It was getting very late in the afternoon and she had no idea how far away they were from a bus stop or a walk back to the hotel.

"I think I know the way from here," Maggie said. "Follow me!"

And so the tired children first marched, then trudged after Maggie as she led them down cobblestone streets, narrow alleys, and twisted snickleways until it was clear that she was lost. To make things worse, it was all but dark. Christina knew Mimi and Papa would be worried, maybe angry with them.

But then they had something more to worry about, because behind them they could hear double heavy footsteps steadily matching their steps. They were being followed!

Run!

"RUN!" Christina screamed suddenly and the kids took off, racing and stumbling their way in the dusk until fortunately they burst out onto a busy street with a big red bus headed their way. As soon as it got to the stop, the children hopped aboard. Christina just hoped it was headed the right way.

As the kids slumped exhaustedly into seats at the back of the bus, Christina asked, "Did anyone have time to turn around and look?"

"Look at what?" said Maggie, in aggravation.

"Didn't you hear the footsteps?" Christina asked.

"I did!" said George.

Grant was strangely silent.

"Grant?" Christina urged. "Did you see anything?"

Grant, who had been last in line, confessed. "I did look behind me real quick."

"AND?!" Christina pleaded, but it was clear Grant did not want to say what he had seen. "You have to tell us," his sister insisted.

Grant blew out a burst of air. "I saw that detective...Sherlock Holmes. He had on that creepy cape and that stupid hat and that big pipe was hanging from his mouth."

"But, Grant," said Maggie. "We told you— Sherlock Holmes is just a fictional character."

"No," said Christina. "If Grant says that's who he saw, then that's who he saw." She believed her little brother. She just didn't understand. As Mimi would say, "the plot thickens."

* * *

Fortunately, the bus was not only going in the right direction, but dropped them off right in front of the Ritz. The bellman whisked them inside. He stood over them, wagging his finger in their faces and Christina thought they must be in big trouble.

"Your Mimi and Papa have a message," he

began. "And your grandfather the same," he added, nodding to Maggie and Grant. "They have gone to a reception at Madame Tussaud's and you are to clean up and join them. Your grandfather brought your clothes over," he told Maggie and George. "I will send you in a taxi."

Whew, thought Christina. She felt sure that they would have gotten a good talking to for being so late if Mimi and Papa had still been here. With no questions asked, she urged the other kids toward the elevator. "We'd better hurry!"

"Who is Madame Tussaud?" asked Grant, once they were on the elevator and headed up to their room. "A friend of Mimi's?"

The other kids laughed and Grant frowned.

"It's ok, Grant," said his sister. "Madame Tussaud's is the famous wax museum."

"Oh, fun," said Grant. "We have to get dressed up to go see *wax*?"

Maggie started to explain, but Christina shushed her. "Let's surprise him!" she whispered and Maggie giggled and nodded.

Soon the kids had dressed and were back downstairs and speeding off in the taxi the bellman had hailed for them.

Grant was curious. "So is this like beeswax? Earwax? Car wax? Furniture polish?" He had everyone giggling, even the driver.

"Just wait and see!" Christina insisted.

When they arrived at Madame Tussaud's, Papa greeted them at the door. "Come in! Come in!" he said. "Mimi has been looking for you, you know. Find her, if you can."

The children hurried inside. They were glad to see that there were tables of snacks and sodas, but Christina assured them that they had better find Mimi first, then eat.

Maggie and George rushed off to find their grandfather. Christina and Grant headed in another direction. There was quite a crowd of people there for the reception and Christina wondered how they would ever find Mimi.

As they waded through room after room, Grant finally tugged at the back of Christina's jacket. "Look at all these famous people," Grant said.

Christina turned. She gave her brother a puzzled look. "You know these people?" she asked, in surprise.

"Don't you!" said Grant. "I saw Elvis Presley and Dr. Martin Luther King, Jr. and William

Shakespeare and even the Queen, but none of them spoke to me." Grant looked thoughtful. "Hey," he added, "aren't some of those people supposed to be dead? And I haven't seen any wax yet."

Christina laughed and gave her brother a hug. "Oh, Grant, believe me—you're seeing gobs and gobs of wax." She waved her arm around. "All these people are made of wax. That's what Madame Tussaud did—she made wax figures of famous people. They look very real, don't they?"

Grant looked like he could hardly believe what his sister was saying. "They look creepy real!" he admitted. "But those guys look way too real!"

Christina turned to see what her wide-eyed brother was looking at. She couldn't be sure, but two of the waiters, in their cutaway tuxedo jackets, looked just like the two guys they had seen at the Globe. Their bushy hair was tied behind their heads in ponytails.

They were serving champagne and canapés from silver trays and had not spotted the children in the crowd.

"Let's go find Mimi and Papa and tell them!" Grant insisted.

"Tell them what?" Christina asked. "We have no proof that these are the Big Ben bombers."

Suddenly, a very large woman that Christina thought might have been a wax figure swished around and accosted her. "WHAT DID YOU SAY, YOUNG LADY?" she demanded of Christina. "WHAT'S THIS ABOUT BIG BEN BEING BOMBED?!"

Instantly, everyone was staring at the two kids. To make things worse, Christina could see Mimi, Papa, and Mr. Byron peeking up over the crowd and trying to make their way forward to see what was going on.

Christina hated being in the spotlight. She had no idea what to say. Grant, on the other hand, was his usual silly self. He began to pose this way and that, as if he were a wax figure trying to get into a proper pose. Some of the adults giggled at Grant's antics. The very large woman stalked off in disgust and the rest of the adults began to wander away as well.

Christina was very relieved, and yet, Mimi and Papa were still headed their way. So was Mr. Byron, with Maggie and George tagging along.

As Mimi approached, Grant grabbed her around her legs which were covered by a beautiful long, black, silky skirt. "Is it really you, Mimi?" Grant teased. He reached up and pinched her rosy cheek as she bent down to hug him. "Is that you, or are you Wax Mimi?"

Everyone laughed and Christina was thrilled to see that none of them appeared to have heard the question the loud woman had been asking. But Mr. Byron had heard. As Mimi and Papa led the kids off to get snacks, Mr. Byron lagged behind with Christina.

As they walked toward the tables filled with food, he whispered to her. "Be careful, Miss Christina," he advised gently. "I have heard rumors myself this very day. It's probably nothing, but you kids need to stay away from Big Ben. Promise?"

When they reached the tables, Christina took a glass of lemonade. As she took a big gulp, she muttered "Prmss" which apparently Mr. Byron took for the word "promise."

But Christina wasn't promising, she was gasping. Why? Because across the table the two bushy-haired waiters were giving her the "evil eye" and the next thing she knew, they had disappeared out a side door.

Her Majesty, the Queen!

The next day was the big day. Mimi was all in a dither and making sure everyone else was too.

"Oh, I hope this is ok to wear," she fussed, trying on her fourth dress of the morning. "I thought I knew what I wanted to wear, but now I'm so confused!"

"Don't get so flustered," Papa soothed her. "It's only the Queen."

"ONLY THE QUEEN?!" Mimi squealed and Christina and Grant burst out laughing.

They had been scrubbed and dressed and groomed, until Grant revolted and ran out into the hallway to escape. Christina was busy practicing her curtsy over and over and over.

Papa looked handsome in his three-piece suit and said he was "cool as a cucumber," but Christina noticed that his forehead was sweaty.

Nonetheless, soon they were all as ready as they ever would be for their audience with the Queen. They had the bellman make their picture before they climbed into the glamorous black town car that Mr. Byron had arranged for them.

"What, no Cinderella carriage?" Grant grumbled, but Christina knew that he was just as excited as she was. It wasn't every day you got to go to a real palace and meet a real, live queen. Butterflies flitted in her tummy.

Christina was thrilled as Buckingham Palace—home of the Queen of England—came into view. She remembered watching the video of the fairytale wedding of Princess Diana. Christina didn't really understand politics yet, she realized, but she knew this was a special moment for them because England had such a long history. In fact, America was sort of still a baby compared to England. Or that's what her social studies teacher had told her.

"Wow!" said Grant, as they entered the grand palace gates. They had arrived just in time to see the famous Changing of the Guard.

They hastened to get out of the car just as the ceremony got underway. Christina thought the pageantry of the black, red, and gold uniforms was grand. She saw Grant making silly faces trying to make the stern-looking guards respond...that is until Papa gave Grant a stern look of his own!

Christina had been to Washington, D.C. and enjoyed her tour of the White House and the nation's Capitol Building. But she thought all this royal grandeur, fancy coaches, flags and pennants, brass horns and drums was even more exciting. Mimi gave her a wink and Christina grinned back.

Soon the ceremony was over and their driver handed them off to an elegant and dapper-looking gentleman who led them toward the palace and their meeting with the Queen. Christina discovered that she was trembling, then she remembered what Mimi had said, "The Queen is just a very nice and smart and talented woman who just happens to be the Queen of England. So just be yourself, be polite, and follow my lead."

Christina repeated this advice to herself under her breath a few times, and the next thing she knew, they were inside the palace and she was making a curtsy IN FRONT OF THE QUEEN!

Grant made a quick, deep bow (and Christina was glad he didn't add any fake funky noises to his performance!), then quickly backed away from the Queen as if she were a mean, old school teacher.

Mimi and Papa beamed proudly. The Queen gave them a big smile and before Christina knew it, Mimi and the Queen were talking non-stop about the value of reading good books, and lamenting that their grandchildren watched too much television and played too many computer games in their spare time.

"But I'm certain these children are dedicated readers," the Queen said, looking right at Grant and Christina.

"Oh, we have to be," Grant volunteered. "Our Mimi writes the books. Besides, we like to catch her mistakes!"

Everyone laughed nervously, except the Queen, who laughed heartily at Grant's sincere confession. "People like to catch my mistakes, too," she admitted back to Grant in a teasing voice.

"Oh, I'm sure a Queen never makes mistakes," Christina blurted, in spite of Mimi's admonition to not speak unless spoken to.

The Queen gave Christina a friendly but serious look...as if they both shared a special secret. "Ohhh," said the Queen. "Everyone makes mistakes...especially young girls who try too hard to solve mysteries in foreign countries."

Christina almost gasped. Mimi and Papa looked puzzled, but before anyone could think too hard about what the Queen had said, their "audience" was over and they were briskly escorted away so that the Queen could meet her next guests.

Back outdoors in the bright sunlight, Christina felt faint. Had she been *warned* by the Queen? Or was Her Royal Highness just teasing her? Strangely, Christina could imagine the Queen as a girl her age, perhaps being rather rambunctious and getting into mild mischief on occasion.

"Hey, Christina," whispered Grant, as they climbed into the back seat of the town car. "I think Queenie has got her eye on you!"

Christina shivered. The Queen. Scotland Yard. Dead defective detectives. Mimi. Papa.

Mr. Byron. Who knows who else? And two shaggy-headed men who were either innocent students, dangerous terrorists, or what?

"My stomach hurts," Christina whined.

"No problem," said Papa. "We're here!"

As they got out of the car, Mimi put her arms around Christina and Grant both and gave them a big hug. "You did a great job!" she said, much to Christina's relief. "It's all over, Christina, and we're going to wash down your butterflies with a big glass of bubbly!"

"You mean we get to drink champagne?!" Grant asked.

"Now what do you think?" Papa asked.

"No way," said Grant. "But I guess you mean we get to drink something cold and fizzy. I can go for that if there are a few chocolate-slathered brownies on the side!"

Papa laughed and held the gate open to the beautiful little garden café by the Thames. Christina was thrilled to see Maggie, George, and Mr. Byron waiting for them at two round tables beneath a beautiful willow tree. She felt better instantly.

"HOW WAS IT?" the three greeted them eagerly.

"I'm soooooooo jealous," drawled Maggie. "I've never met the Queen." She gave her grandfather a "look."

"Well, maybe when I get to be made a knight, you can meet her," he teased. "Of course, you'll have to call me Sir, then!"

George groaned. "We have to call you sir, now!"

Mr. Byron roared. "But then you'd have to call me Sir Grand Dad!"

Everyone laughed and sat down, and the adults began to talk about the exciting events of the day at their larger table. Quickly, the four kids scooted their chairs close together around their smaller table and began to compare notes.

"The Queen fussed at Christina!" Grant told right off.

"Did not!" Christina countered.

"Did, too!" Grant said, shaking his head up and down at the other two kids.

They piled their plates full of tiny cucumber sandwiches, teacakes, scones, and something Maggie said was clotted cream and munched away hungrily. Tall, fizzy, pink drinks with colorful paper parasols and thin red straws were set down by the waitress.

"What did she actually say?" Maggie asked eagerly. "Will your name be on the front of the newspaper?"

"Will you be on the nightly news?" George asked hopefully.

Christina stomped her foot on the grass beneath the table. "No way! She just said I should not be such an eager-beaver mystery-solver," she paraphrased.

"The Queen said 'eager-beaver,'" George asked doubtfully.

"Hush, George!" said Maggie. "That's beside the point." Then she turned to Christina seriously. "Do you think the Queen has heard the same rumors that grandfather has? He's been on the phone a lot with that Scotland Yard detective. I don't know what's up, but he won't let us out of his sight!"

Last Warning!

Later that night, Christina grew very somber. They were back at the Ritz. Maggie and George were getting to spend the night in their large suite. The adults had gone to some gala at the Tate Museum. Mimi and Papa were big on galas. Mimi was still on cloud nine after having met the Queen.

Christina was exhausted and had a headache. The boys were watching cartoons in their pajamas in another room. Maggie just sat waiting for Christina to perk up. "What's wrong?" she asked her American friend.

Christina rubbed her head. "I'm not sure," she confessed. "It's just that the adults have shut us out of this mystery, if there is indeed one. It's like they want us to get lost while they solve the mystery—if there is one. And yet they act like there is no mystery...that we're just kids being silly, causing trouble."

Maggie sighed and held her friend's hand. "I think they just want us to be safe. We are kids, after all. And bombs are dangerous things."

"I know," said Christina. "But they won't even listen to us. Maybe we are wrong, but what if we are right? What if Big Ben really is in danger? A bomb could hurt people...not to mention destroy an historic clock."

The girls looked up, surprised to see Grant standing in the doorway. He was almost in tears. "Oh, there is a m-m-mystery," he said, his voice quivering.

Grant had taken a nap when they got back to the hotel after tea, and Christina thought he must have had a bad dream, or maybe something on those stupid battle cartoons frightened him. "What is it, Grant?" she asked gently.

Reluctantly, Grant pulled a piece of paper out of his back pocket. "I found this," he said. "In the back of the town car after we left the café. I guess someone tossed it in there." He handed his sister the wadded note. "I didn't want to tell you because I didn't want the Queen to come and lock you up in a dungeon if you did anything about it." A single tear trickled down his cheek. Christina could tell he was truly afraid.

She looked down and read the note aloud to all of them, including George who had followed Grant into the room.

TO THE KIDS WHO KEEP FOLLOWING US AROUND:
   IT WOULD BE VERY DANGEROUS FOR YOU TO GO BACK TO BIG BEN TONIGHT BEFORE MIDNIGHT. MIND YOUR BUSINESS AND STAY SAFE. INTERFERE AT YOUR PERIL. DO NOT, REPEAT, DO NOT GO TO BIG BEN TONIGHT.
   REMEMBERETH WHAT WE SAY AND MINDETH THAT YOU STAY AWAY!
   LAST WARNING!

"Wow!" said Christina. "This means that whatever is going to happen is going to happen TONIGHT! Maybe we are too late!"

Maggie shook Christina by her shoulders. "Christina, this is not one of your grandmother's kids' mysteries—this is real life. We can't go to Big Ben."

"We can call granddad and tell him," George suggested. Before the others could respond, he grabbed the telephone and dialed Mr. Byron's cell phone number. When he did not answer, George left a message: "MEET US AT BIG BEN RIGHT AWAY!"

"Try Mimi and Papa!" Grant urged his sister. Christina grabbed the phone and dialed their cell number that she knew by heart. There was no answer and she figured that the cell phones didn't work inside that building, because Mimi or Papa always answered. When the recorded message ended, Christina pleaded into the phone: 'MIMI, PAPA, WE CAN'T HELP IT...WE'VE GOT TO SAVE BIG BEN...MEET US THERE BEFORE MIDNIGHT!"

When she put down the phone, she stared at the others. "Well," she said gravely, "do we have to try to save Big Ben, or not? Grant, you could stay here."

"No way!" squealed Grant, slapping his hands on his hips. "I was the first one to see those guys and that scribbling on the clock tower," he reminded them. "I'm not afraid. Let's go before we're too late! If the Queen doesn't like it, well, well, well," Grant sputtered, "she just might have to buy herself a watch for Christmas!"

Trick...or Treat?

If the regular bell captain had been on duty, he probably would have stopped them. After all, it was after eleven o'clock at night. But there was a new, young bellman on duty, and he opened the door grandly and hailed a taxi for the kids, as they requested.

"I have just enough money left," Maggie said, counting out the pound notes in her pocket.

The foursome made quite a sight to anyone paying attention: Christina still had on her "meet the Queen" outfit...Maggie wore jeans and a cut-off tee shirt...George (not even thinking about it) was dressed in the Superman pajamas he had put on to watch cartoons...and Grant was buried somewhere under one of Mimi's caped houndstooth jackets; he also wore her new deerstalker cap, and had grabbed the large magnifying glass Papa used to open the mail. They looked more like trick-or-treaters than desperate kids on a frightening mission—save Big Ben!

"Do your parents know you're heading out this late?" the cabbie asked them.

"They do now," Christina said, forlornly. No telling if the adults would get the phone messages and meet them, or what trouble the kids would be in if they did.

Maggie asked for the cabbie to drop them off across and just down the street from the clock tower. As they climbed out of the taxi, the kids noticed that it had begun to trickle rain. The taxi's red taillights left what looked like a seeping trail of blood on the dark, wet street. Gaslights along the street threw out eerie shadows. No one was about. Or so it seemed.

"Look!" Grant whispered loudly. "Up there!"

The other kids turned their gaze up to the face of the clock. Behind the glowing light they could see shadows moving around. The bad guys?!

"We have to get up there—fast!" Christina said.

"What if the bomb goes off?" Maggie asked, holding back.

"We came to stop that from happening, remember?" Christina said, much more bravely than she felt. Inside her chest, her heart beat like a vibrating drum.

"There are probably a lot of steps," George reminded them.

"Then we'd better get started," urged Grant. He took off across the street, cape flying. The others followed and once they got inside the clock tower, they flew up the stairs, trying to be quiet as mice. "Don't you see!" he said, glancing one last time at the illuminated clock face, "It's almost midnight!"

As they got near the area of the clock face, they slowed down to a tiptoe. Christina was the first to peer into the clock tower room. She could not believe how large the gigantic round moon faces of the clock were. Why the minute hand was at least twice as long as Papa was tall! She felt like Alice in Wonderland...very small near the amazing clock.

The other kids crowded behind her. The clock ticked forward—and what was silent when they were down below seemed to make a great noise when they were so close to it.

George pointed to the two backpacks stuffed in the corner. "The bombs?" he hissed.

Christina glanced at the clock, having some difficulty trying to tell time from the inside out. "I think we have time to get them downstairs!"

She ran forward and grabbed one of the backpacks. Grant did the same.

"NO!" screamed Maggie. "Too dangerous!!"

"Hey, who's there?" a gruff voice called up to them from below.

"Get outta here!" a second voice demanded.

There was no time to think. Christina and Grant—backpacks slung over their shoulders—raced back down the steps JUST AS THE CLOCK BEGAN TO STRIKE TWELVE!

"No time," screamed Maggie, who had run on ahead.

"Look!" cried George. He had stopped on a landing where there was a small room. Maggie stopped to grab her brother and shove him down the staircase, but he would not budge.

"No!" George insisted. "I read about this room. It's an old cell. Look inside!"

Grant and Christina had been forced to stop since Maggie and George blocked the way.

The great clock continued its outrageous *bong bong bong*.

The four kids peered into the dark room. The two men were cowering inside, trying to hide. Once they realized they'd been found, they burst forward toward the door, screaming, "Get out of here, you kids!"

"Quick, Grant" Christina shrieked. *Bong*. "Throw your backpack inside!" *Bong*. Grant threw the backpack as hard as he could. It hit one man in the leg and he howled and slowed down. *Bong*. Christina threw her backpack with all her might. It hit the other man in the stomach and with an *"Ooff!"* he slouched forward and fell down right at the door.

As quickly as they could...*bong*...the four kids slammed the cell door closed and locked it...*bong*. Then everyone stood absolutely still. The two men lolled on the floor, grasping at the cell door. The kids held their hands over their mouths.

Bong...bong ...BONG! Then...silence.

For what was only seconds, but seemed like hours, the kids remained frozen in place.

Finally, Grant found his voice, which quavered, "C-c-christina, the bombs didn't go off?"

Christina could hardly speak back. "No... not yet?"

"Midnight's come and gone," Maggie whispered hopefully.

"What are you laughing at?" George asked the two men angrily. "This isn't funny!"

"Wow," said Grant, "neither is this," he added as they heard a lot of noise down below. "Here come the bombs that are gonna go off!"

Sure enough, they all could hear Mimi, Papa, Mr. Byron, and many other voices as the crowd clomped up the stairs, calling their names.

"We're here!" cried Christina. She knew her grandmother must be petrified. She wondered how long she and Grant would be on "restriction" for this.

"We're ok!" Maggie called loudly.

"It's all over!" George cried down to them.

"OH NO IT'S NOT!" bellowed Papa, first to reach the scene. "WHAT IS GOING ON HERE?!" he demanded in the angriest voice Christina had ever heard him use.

Saved by the Bell!

"Big Ben's ok," Grant squeaked. His (Mimi's) cape draped all around him on the dusty floor. His (Mimi's) hat was "cockamamie" on his head. He held the large magnifying glass up to his face as if he wished he could hide behind it.

Mimi grabbed Grant in a bear hug embrace. "Of course Big Ben's ok," she said. "And so are you?" she asked, her voice trembling. She looked at Christina.

"Yes, Mimi, we're all ok," Christina promised her grandmother, who grabbed her next and smothered her with kisses.

Mr. Byron held Maggie and George with both

arms. Christina thought she heard one big joint sigh of relief.

But Papa glared at the two men. So did the policemen who had followed them up the stairs.

"Who would like to start explaining first?" Papa said, and the bobbies pulled out their notepads...and their handcuffs.

* * *

It took a long, long time to get all the explaining done. First the kids told how they had first spotted the shaggy-headed men with their suspicious backpacks and saw the scribbled sketch on the side of the clock tower.

Then the two men—very young men, actually—explained (over and over) how they weren't terrorists, but college students. "We're not terrorists!" one insisted. "We are studying to be actors and film directors. We are just making a movie," the other one swore.

"And you had permission to make your movie at midnight inside of Big Ben's clock tower?" the chief detective demanded.

"No," admitted one of the students. "That's why we tried to scare these kids away. We were afraid they would tell."

"I mean every time we turned around—there they were!" said the other man.

"How could that be?" asked Mr. Byron. But once they went back over many of the facts, it turned out to just be curious coincidences that the actors were also waiters, working as substitutes the night the kids had been at the reception at Madame Tussaud's Wax Museum.

"And you just happened to be at the Globe when we were there?" Christina asked incredulously.

"I said we're actors," the first man said. "We were checking on auditions."

"We thought you were following us!" Maggie said.

"Well, we thought you were following us!!" the man retorted.

The second man confessed, "We were even working at the outdoor café you came to for tea, but you never saw us. That's when we put that note in the town car, trying to scare you away one last time."

Finally Papa and the police had heard enough. Christina knew Papa well enough that kids making a mistake was one thing, but grown men (even if they were just college students) making mistakes like breaking and entering and scaring little kids was serious stuff, not funny at all.

The police must have felt the same way because they opened the cell door, slapped the students in handcuffs, confiscated the backpacks filled with camera equipment, and read them their rights as they hauled them down the long flight of stairs.

That left four kids standing and staring—in fear and trembling—at three exhausted and exasperated adults.

Elementary, My Dear Watson!

The next morning, the kids and adults were gathered around one large table in the glamorous Ritz dining room having their last breakfast together. It would be time to leave for the airport shortly.

Grant had returned Mimi's cape and given her the deerslayer hat which she wore jauntily on her head. Mimi loved hats.

"Well, this has been quite an adventurous week for all concerned," said Mr. Byron.

"We're sorry if we caused any trouble," Christina said. "And I really hope those two college kids don't get in too much trouble."

Mr. Byron smiled. "Well, it's hard to fault

you children for trying to protect England's most famous landmark."

Mimi nodded in agreement, then frowned. "But never again!" she wanted the kids to promise. "You're not characters in a book, you know—one of these days you're going to get into serious trouble, trouble you can't get out of."

Christina shook her head back and forth rapidly. "No more terrorists or bombs or anything like that for me," she promised.

Mr. Byron stared at his grandchildren from beneath arched eyebrows. "Us either!" Maggie and George promised.

"Graaaaant?" Papa said.

Grant squirmed in his seat. "Well, I don't know...I sorta like being Sherlock Holmesy...but if I never hear another clock *BONG!* up close and personal, it will be fine with me. I think I'm deaf!"

"GRAAAAANT!" Papa repeated.

"Alright! Alright!" Grant gave in. "No solving stupid mysteries or stuff like that."

Suddenly the bell captain appeared in front of them with a silver tray held in his gloved hand. "For you, I believe," he said to the children. He thrust the tray forward and Christina picked up the envelope that sat upon it.

"What's that?" Mimi asked suspiciously.

"I don't know," Christina promised. She looked down at the beautiful envelope with the gold embossed crown on it. Carefully, with the other kids hovered around her, she opened the envelope and pulled out a small piece of notepaper.

As the other kids crouched even closer over her shoulders, Christina opened the note. Silently the kids read the note to themselves. One by one they began to smile.

"Cool!" said Maggie.

"Wow!" said Christina.

"Who'da thunk it?" said George.

Grant grinned biggest of them all, but said nothing.

"Well?" said Mr. Byron.

"Well!" said Papa.

"WELL?!" said Mimi. "Don't keep us in suspense. What does the note say? Who is it from?"

Christina turned the note around and placed it on the table in front of the adults. "It's from the Queen," she said proudly. "Thanking us for 'saving Big Ben.'"

The adults gasped as they passed the note

from one to the other.

Grant stood up and stretched and yawned. "Well I think I'll just go up and write Old Queenie back," he said.

"And say what?" demanded Mimi.

Grant smiled. "It's elementary, my dear Watson. I'll say I'm sure glad that she doesn't have to buy a dumb old watch for Christmas after all."

The adults frowned and the kids giggled. The bell captain reappeared. "If you're ready to go to the airport," he said directly to the kids, "your carriage awaits."

"What is it this time?" asked Grant. "Another spooky old black town car?"

The bell captain huffed, "I said your CARRIAGE awaits."

First Christina and Maggie stared at one another with big eyes. Then Grant and George looked at one another with big O mouths.

"You don't think?..." Christina began.

"We'd better go see!" Maggie finished and the four children ran from the table knocking scones and cream pots this way and that.

"You don't *really* think..." Mimi started.

"*We'd* better go see!" Papa and Mr. Byron

said, and like kids themselves, they dashed out of the dining room, leaving the bell captain standing there with a big grin on his face.

The BONG! End

CHICAGO HEIGHTS PUBLIC LIBRARY